ARNIE
Goes to Camp

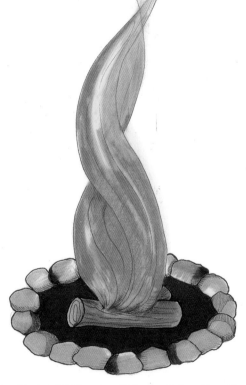

NANCY CARLSON

VIKING KESTREL

Dedicated to the Minnesota Outward Bound school.
The experience changed my life.

VIKING KESTREL
Viking Penguin Inc., 40 West 23rd Street, New York, New York 10010, U.S.A.
Penguin Books Ltd, 27 Wrights Lane, London W8 5TZ (Publishing & Editorial) and
Harmondsworth, Middlesex, England (Distribution & Warehouse)
Penguin Books Australia Ltd, Ringwood, Victoria, Australia
Penguin Books Canada Limited, 2801 John Street, Markham, Ontario, Canada L3R 1B4
Penguin Books (N.Z.) Ltd, 182–190 Wairau Road, Auckland 10, New Zealand

Copyright © Nancy Carlson, 1988
All rights reserved
First published in 1988 by Viking Penguin Inc.
Published simultaneously in Canada
Printed in Japan by Dai Nippon Printing Co. Ltd.
Set in Clarendon Book

1   2   3   4   5   92   91   90   89   88

Library of Congress Cataloging-in-Publication Data
Carlson, Nancy L.   Arnie goes to camp / by Nancy Carlson.
p.   cm.
Summary: Arnie is sure that he won't survive summer sleepaway
camp: but when he arrives he is surprised to find that camp is not
at all what he expected.
ISBN 0-670-81549-7
[1. Camps—Fiction.]   I. Title.   PZ7.C21665At   1988   [E]—dc19   87-19868

One summer Arnie's mom decided to send him to sleep-away camp.

"I don't think I'll like camp," said Arnie. "It's only for two weeks," said Mom. "You'll love it!"

But Arnie wasn't so sure.

The day he left for camp it was raining.
All the other kids seemed to know each other.

On the bus everyone sang silly songs. Arnie
didn't know the words. He just stared out
the window, as the bus went further and
further from his home.

When they arrived at camp, Arnie met his
counselor Stretch. Stretch was eighteen years old
and wore all sorts of camping gear on his belt.
"Stretch is kind of neat," Arnie thought.

When they all hiked to their cabin, Arnie
thought of his mom. He felt like crying.

Arnie's bunk-mate was a kid named Ted.
Ted liked to play tricks. Arnie thought of his
friend Louanne. He missed her.

Suddenly a bell rang. "Oh boy, it's lunch!"
yelled Ted. Everyone rushed off.
"I'm not hungry," thought Arnie.

But when Arnie sat down, he saw lunch was hot dogs and beans. "My favorite!" he said.

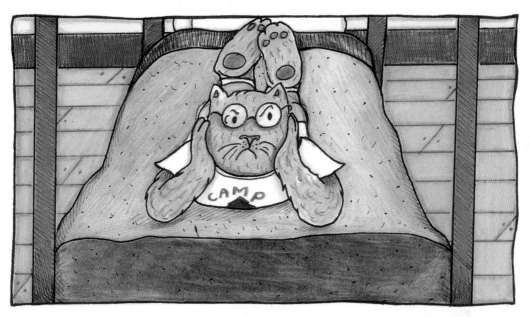

After lunch Stretch made everyone take a nap.
"I'm too old for a nap," Arnie complained.

But all during nap-time Ted goofed off and
made everyone laugh. "He's funny," thought Arnie.

After nap-time Stretch told everyone to get ready for a hike. "I won't like this," grumbled Arnie. But the hike was fun. Arnie had never seen such neat things. He even held a snake.

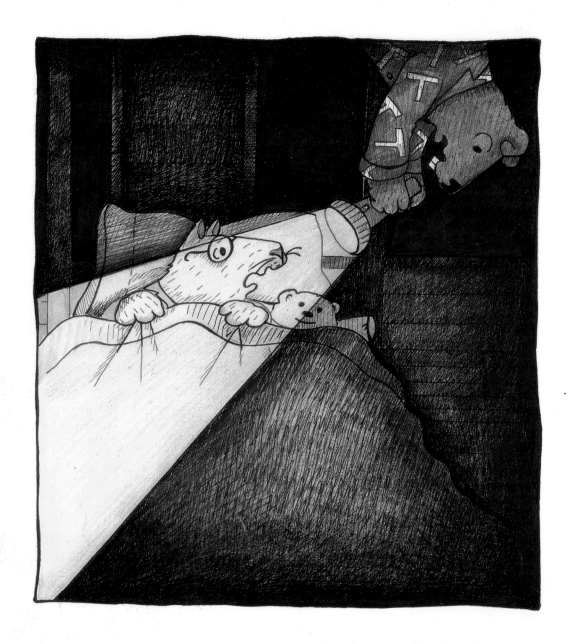

When it was time for bed, Arnie was scared.
Suddenly there was a "hoo-hoo-hoo."
"Did you hear that?" asked Ted.

"It's a wild animal!" said Arnie. "Stretch!"
yelled everyone in the cabin. Stretch got up
and showed them it was just a friendly owl.

All week long Arnie hardly had time to think of home. At night they all sat around the campfire. Arnie heard lots of scary stories and learned lots of new songs.

One day Ted and Arnie put a frog in Stretch's bed.

Arnie learned new games at camp. His
favorite was capture the flag.

Arnie went to Arts and Crafts, and he went canoeing.

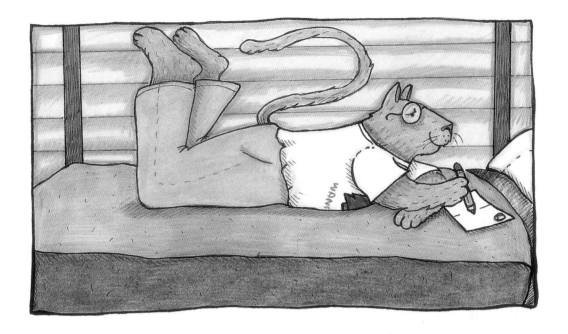

Twice a week Stretch made everyone write
letters home.

Arnie thought camp was really great, until
the day he and Ted found a beehive.

The bee stings really hurt. But after the camp nurse took care of them, Arnie and Ted felt much better.

Arnie had learned so many new things at camp.

He couldn't believe the two weeks were almost over.

The last day of camp Arnie got the "Best New Camper" award. Ted got the "Biggest Trickster" award.

When it was time to leave camp, Arnie felt a
little sad. He gave Stretch a big hug.

He gave Ted his address. "I'm sure going to
miss your jokes!" Arnie said.

All the way home on the bus Arnie sang silly songs, the loudest one of all!!!